# Lola Flies Alone

written by **Bill Richardson**
&
illustrated by **Bill Pechet**

At last! The day had dawned when, for the very first time, Lola would fly alone. It was a Special Occasion.

Special Occasions require Special Outfits. Lola considered carefully. She chose her lime-coloured mermaid leggings, sparkly and scaly and with flappy fins at the ankles; her ballerina tutu, rose-coloured and puffy; and her red velvet cape to which were attached peach-coloured fairy wings. The wings came with a magic wand; what good would be fairy wings without such an accessory? Lola completed the ensemble with her sky-blue ball cap atop which sat a unicorn horn. It was unicorn-coloured.

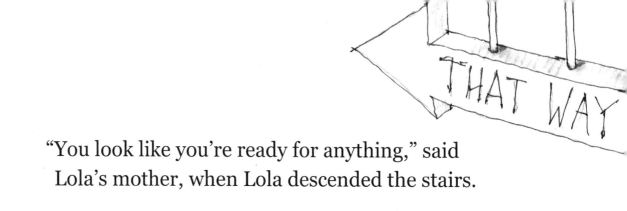

"You look like you're ready for anything," said Lola's mother, when Lola descended the stairs.

"Indeed I am," said Lola.

At the airport, Lola's mother said, "Do you remember the Traveling Alone Pledge?"

This was a Code of Conduct Lola's mother had invented; she was that nervous kind of person who found such oaths reassuring. Lola raised her right hand and spoke with due solemnity.

"I shall be good and kind and generous and brave."

"Give Gran some of my love and keep the rest
for yourself," said Lola's mother, gathering
her into her arms.

Lola could tell she was trying hard not to cry,
and therefore didn't squirm, even though
the hugging was so vigorous she worried
for the puffiness of her tutu and the fragility
of her wings.

ADVENTURE
AWAITS

Lola was the first passenger to board the plane. Arshbir was waiting for her. Arshbir was the flight attendant.

"I love, love, really love your outfit, Lola. Are those mermaid leggings?"

Lola confirmed this with a nod.

"I wish I had a pair just like them," said Arshbir.

Lola didn't think mermaid leggings would much suit Arshbir, but to say so would neither have been good nor kind nor generous nor brave, so she gave him a nod that didn't say much at all.

"Have you flown alone before?"

"It is my first time."

"Don't worry. It's easy. And anyway, you look like you're ready for anything."

Lola said, "Indeed I am."

Arshbir took Lola to 13A. She allowed him
to show her how to fasten the seat belt, even
though she already knew, thanks to some helpful
YouTube videos. He also demonstrated how
to press the call button, should assistance
be required.

"Can you reach it? It's quite high up."

"I'll use my magic wand."

"Excellent plan. I'll leave you to get settled. The other passengers are waiting to board the plane."

"Travel is tiring," said Lola to herself, as Arshbir walked away. "Perhaps I'll treat myself to the shortest visit to Napland."

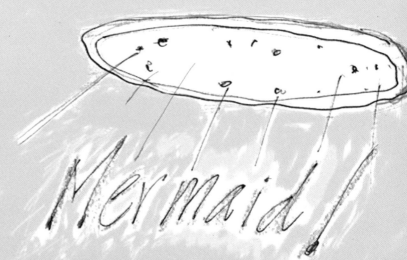

But hardly had she closed her eyes,
when she heard Arshbir make an announcement
on the loud speaker.

"Excuse me, is there a mermaid on board? We
have an emergency only a mermaid can handle.
If you're a mermaid, please press the call button."

Lola seized her wand and pressed. Arshbir hurried
to 13A.

"Lola! Of course, you're a mermaid! What should we do?"

He pointed out the window. Lola looked and saw that some other mermaids, all of them very merry, had set up a big wading pool, and were splashing and laughing and shouting and having so much raucous fun they didn't even notice they were smack dab in the middle of the runway, and were keeping the plane from taking off.

"I'll take care of that," said Lola, who beamed
a message out of her mermaid eyes that only
other mermaids could detect. "Be good! If you
don't move your wading pool, this plane will be
stuck here forever!"

The mermaids heard her right away.
They understood. They gave her
a jolly wave, packed up their pool,
and hurried away to continue
their moist merrymaking
in a more convenient locale.

EMERGENCY!

Lola returned to Napland, but not for long. Soon, she was wakened by another announcement from Arshbir on the loud speaker.

"Excuse me, is there a ballerina on board? We have an emergency only a ballerina can handle. If you're a ballerina, please press the call button."

Lola seized her wand and pressed. Arshbir hurried to 13A.

"Lola! Of course, you're a ballerina! What should we do?"

He pointed to where another ballerina, whose tutu was even poofier than Lola's, was practicing her demi-pliés and arabesques right in the middle of the aisle. None of the passengers could get past her to find their seats.

"I'll take care of that," said Lola, who pirouetted to where the ballerina was clogging everything up with her antics.

*Madama Tilda Von-Tutu*

"Be kind," Lola said to the ballerina, very firmly. "If you keep dancing here, no one can sit down, no one can buckle their seat belts, and we won't be able to take off."

"Well, I never!" said the ballerina, huffily. She didn't give a stale fig for being kind, but as she could see that Lola was ready for anything and would brook no resistance, she stalked off in a huff.

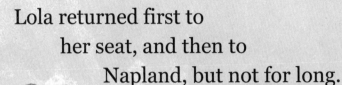

Lola returned first to
her seat, and then to
Napland, but not for long.
Soon, she was
wakened by another
announcement
from Arshbir
on the loud speaker.

"Excuse me, is there
a fairy on board? We have
an emergency only a fairy can handle.
If you're a fairy, please press the call button."

Lola seized her wand and pressed. Arshbir hurried
to 13A.

"Lola! Of course, you're a fairy! What should we do?"

He pointed to the front of the plane where a very greedy fairy was eating all the crustless egg salad sandwiches Arshbir had made to serve the passengers, many of whom were ravenous.

"I'll take care of that," said Lola, who spread
    her fairy wings and flew in the blink of an eye
to where the greedy fairy stuffed and gobbled.

"Be generous," said Lola. "If you eat all the
sandwiches, everyone else on the plane will
    go hungry."

"What if I don't want to be generous?"
said the greedy fairy, most peevishly.

"Then I will turn YOU into a sandwich," said Lola,
waving her magic wand, "or a pickle, and
someone will eat you up!"

The fairy saw that Lola was ready for anything.
She shrieked and vanished, leaving behind
an unfortunate waft of rotten egg.

Lola returned first to to her seat, and then to Napland, but not for long. Soon, she was wakened by another announcement from Arshbir on the loud speaker.

"Excuse me, is there a unicorn on board? We have an emergency only a unicorn can handle. If you're a unicorn, please press the call button."

Lola seized her wand and pressed. Arshbir hurried to 13A.

"Lola! Of course, you're a unicorn! What should we do?"

He pointed to where a little girl sat all by herself, forlorn and weeping. Lola joined her.

"What's wrong?"

"I forgot my lucky unicorn at home and I am flying alone for the first time and I don't feel ready for anything!"

"Well," said Lola, "I happen to be a unicorn."

"And are you lucky?" asked the girl.

"So far."

"And are you ready for anything?"

"Indeed I am," said Lola. "If I sat beside you, would you feel brave?"

"I would," said the girl.

The girl closed her eyes. So did Lola. She returned to Napland. She enjoyed its beautiful views and many surprising events.

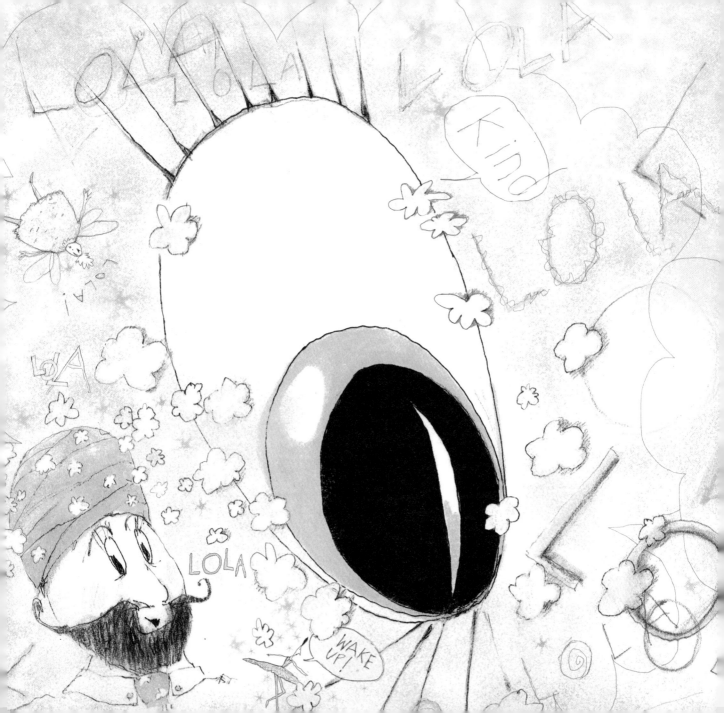

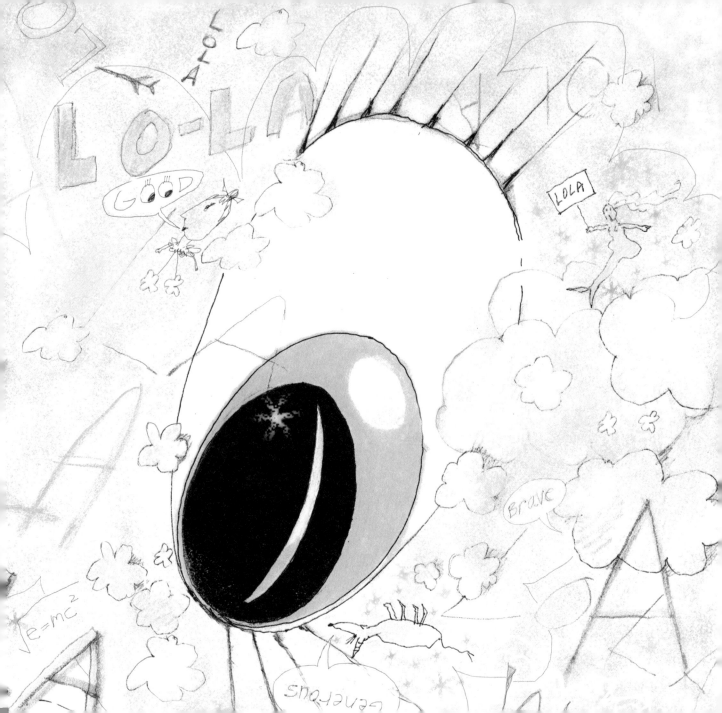

The next time she opened her eyes, it was again because she heard Arshbir's voice—not on the loud speaker, but right beside her.

"Lola. Lola. Time to wake up. I hope you enjoyed your first flight alone."

"It hasn't happened yet!" Lola said.

"It surely has. You were Sleeping Beauty the whole time. See? All the other passengers have left. You were to first to board, and you'll be the last to leave."

Stuff and nonsense!
Lola was poised to remind
him of the mermaids and
the ballerina and the fairy
and the little girl
who missed her unicorn.
But then she saw Gran
hurrying down the aisle
of the empty plane.

"Lola!"

"Gran!"

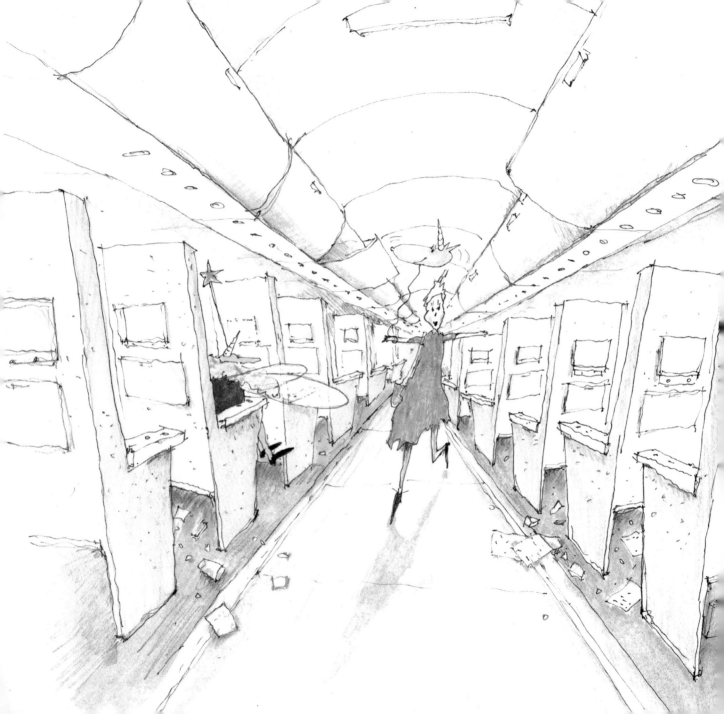

They hugged like two people who love each other and haven't met for a long time, which, in fact, they were.

"Were you good and kind and generous and brave?" Gran asked. No doubt Lola's mother had put her up to it.

"Without hesitation or fail," Lola said.

Gran said, "I have so much planned for us to do," and as they made their way to the exit she began to list off all the activities she had in mind, some of them quite rigorous. Lola was not concerned. Lola took it all in stride. About Lola, nothing was flappable except her wings. Lola was ready for anything. Indeed she was.

LOLA + GRAN RIDE A CAMEL

LOLA + GRAN' HAVE RAMEN

LOLA + GRAN GO HIKING

LOLA + GRAN GO CANOEING

LOLA + GRAN GO TO THE OPERA

This book was designed by Veselina Tomova of Vis-à-Vis Graphics,
St. John's, NL, and printed in Canada.

9781927917831

Running the Goat, Books & Broadsides gratefully acknowledges support
for its publishing activities from Newfoundland and Labrador's Department
of Tourism, Culture, Arts and Recreation through its Publishers Assistance
Program; the Department of Canadian Heritage through the Canada Book Fund;
and the Canada Council for the Arts,
through its Literary Publishing Projects Fund.

For dreamers everywhere

*Lola Flies Alone*